EFFORTLESS LOVE

KHARY H. TOLLIVER

First printing

ISBN- 9798513507178
Printed in the United States of America

This book is dedicated to a couple that has shown and proven to me what everlasting love is.

Ernest and Mattie Mae Manigo

I would like to express a very special thank you to Miss. A. Reed, Mrs. S. Chebowski, Miss. C. Jennier and Mrs. S. Hardin Olexy.

Effortless love. Effortless, is how any **true love** should be. From being drawn to each other, then confirming your relationship, to effortlessly falling in love. I believe that true love, will not need a lot of effort to do anything. You should both be willing to do anything it takes to keep your love going effortlessly. Yes, sometimes there may be a sacrifice or some compromise, but it should be done, effortlessly. As I will always continue to say, no relationship is perfect, but it must be well worth it. The love poems in this book are expressions of effortless love, praising love, adoring love and love that is more than well worth it. These are poems from my poem journal, poems that come from my heart, experiences that I've expressed, beautiful experiences that I've seen and beautiful thoughts that I sometimes have. The relationship affirmations in this book are just **MY** thoughts and opinions, they are not facts. I am no relationship specialist and I'm far from an expert on relationships. I do hope to touch souls with these poems and affirmations. I hope they warm hearts, give ideas, inspire and most of all, I hope they make you want to be in love or appreciate the love you already have. A beautiful love is an effortless love.

Khary H Tolliver

TABLE OF CONTENTS

RELATIONSHIP AFFIRMATIONS

EVERLASTING LOVE

What we have in our love, is so many beautiful
things,
now I'm going from store to store, looking at
wedding rings.
yes, that's what's on my mind,
because I've known, what I have is a rare find.

After falling deep in love with you,
I just knew, no other woman could ever do.
I adore how you constantly assure your love for me,
beautifully, verbally, and physically.

Learning each other's love language from the start,
made it easy to capture each other's heart.
It was so easy to love each other,
but we're not perfect, sometimes we argue like
sister and brother.

Yes, we have some ups and downs, but we still
make it,
as long as God is in our love, we're going to always
make it.
With God in our love it's easy,
as we continue to love on each other, effortlessly.

Still, whenever I look into your pretty eyes, I see
forever,
and I just know, even if I tried, I couldn't have done
any better.
We bring so much joy to each other, people say
we're beautiful,
so much love, to some it's unusual.

My heart has never been so happy,
because we have a beautiful everlasting love, like
Ernest and Mattie.
As we continue to grow in love, it just gets greater,
all thanks to our creator.

Our December kiss during the Sagittarius season,
yes, you hunted this hunter down for a beautiful
reason.
Since then, you're all I've ever been thinking of,
now look at what we have, this everlasting love.

A SPECIAL KIND OF LOVE

I wake up every morning looking forward to kissing
your lips,
I promise you, I've never been in love like this.
What we have, I'm very sure of,
it's a very special kind of love.

You're the only woman who's ever touched my
heart with a conversation,
being with you, wherever we are, is pure relaxation,
because you have me constantly on cloud nine,
finally, an angel that's all mine.

You're such a beautiful blessing,
constantly, my feelings are progressing.
You're a dream come true,
and I've always dreamed of loving someone, just
like you.

I'll always put you first,
I'll be there for you at your best and at your worst,
because I know that's what you'll do for me,
in love forever, that's how it's going to be.

Nothing but good times and lots of laughter,
love, joy and happiness, seems like that's what
we're both after.
You're such an amazing woman,
and I'm so glad to have you as, my woman.

You make me feel like a king,
with all the special things you do for me, you make
my heart sing,
so please don't ever stop giving me your love,
because it's such, a special kind of love.

SHE'S SPEAKING MY LOVE LANGUAGE

My love, bless her beautiful heart,
she's been speaking my love language from the
start.
My love language is not complicated, it's very easy
to speak,
the way she speaks it, sometimes it makes me weak.

She starts speaking my language, with that quality
time,
no doubt, she's my partner in crime.
We do so many great things together,
and each day, it just gets better and better.

She speaks my language, with those words of
affirmation,
by telling me how she feels about me, with no
hesitation.
She expresses her feelings for me with ease,
that's why one day I'll be proposing to her, on both
knees.

Then she speaks the favorite part of my language,
that physical touch,
hers, have mercy, I just adore, and crave so much.
I love when she kisses me or touches any part of my
body,
and always, when she makes love to me.

I love speaking her love language too,
it's easy, because my love for her is true.
Effortlessly, we speak each other's love language,
and I love listening when, she's speaking my love
language.

MY WONDERFUL WOMAN

She puts her arms around me and chases my worries
away,
she's my ribbon in the sky on a beautiful day.
Wherever she is, that's my happy place,
that's anywhere I can receive her warm embrace.

I know we're headed in the right direction,
because she's always giving me so much love and
affection.
I love reminiscing about our innocent beginning,
the day I committed to her, I knew there would
never be an ending.

I was happy before this wonderful woman came
into my life,
now I'm ecstatic and everything feels just right.
They say a love like this is nonexistent,
I bet my life we go more than just the distance.

She's such a beautiful and happy soul,
she's the one, together we're going to grow old,
and I couldn't have asked for a better woman,
she's so amazing, my wonderful woman.

EFFORTLESS LOVE

This relationship is blessed from above,
it's beautiful, it's an effortless love,
because it's God sent, and we're so blessed,
in this love, neither one of us is ever stressed.

Giving the glory always to God of course, we're
both so thankful,
for blessing us with a love, that's so effortlessly
wonderful.
Praying with my best friend and lover,
never any worries, because we've assured our love
to each other.

We don't just love each other,
we are, in love, with each other,
and both wholeheartedly, know this love is heaven
sent,
because we both effortlessly give, one hundred
percent.

It takes no effort to tell her, always, I love her,
and it takes no effort for me to, always, hold and
kiss her.
She effortlessly, always reciprocates,
it's a love that we both deserve and appreciate.

We know each other's worth,
for us, our love is the most important thing on this
earth.
Our attraction started from knowing what was
inside, in the beginning,
because beauty is skin deep, we both came out
winning.

Even though every box may not be checked,
we're both fine knowing that this love will never be
perfect.
We know for good reasons, God has brought us
together,
with flaws and all, nothing else can be better.

Neither one of us wants for anything,
but each other, and it's inevitable, I'll be blessing
her with that ring.
There is no trying to make this work, because it's
blessed from above,
and there's just no hard work at all, in what we
have, effortless love.

THE SWEETEST LOVE EVER

My love, I'm so very thankful for you,
through the ups and downs, you've always
remained true.
No matter what, you stayed by my side,
giving me the sweetest love ever, as we endure this
wonderful ride.

I never thought I'd be with someone who's just as
affectionate as I am,
passionate about our relationship and truly
appreciates me as their man.
Love, that is all you,
and I just love you so much, you know I truly do.

After all this time, you always assure me that you're
still interested in me,
and thank you for letting me know, that's how it's
always going to be.
You always give me your undivided attention,
because you're in love with me, between us, we
rarely have any tension.

I love all the sweet pet names you have for me:
handsome, honey, baby, and sometimes even, sweet
daddy.
You really know how to make me feel good,
as I reciprocate the same sweetness for you, because
I love you and I really should.

I love the way you randomly touch me, kiss me,
hold me,
make love to me, and when I'm not around, you
truly miss me.
That just makes me adore you even more,
woman, I'm not ever going anywhere, that's for
sure.

I appreciate the delicious home cooked meals you
make,
and the way you show that you care for me – girl,
you're just as sweet as birthday cake.
You truly are the best girlfriend ever,
please don't ever stop giving me, the sweetest love
ever.

I JUST WANTED YOU TO KNOW

Your undivided attention means the world to me,
your hugs and kisses, they mean the world to me.
All of your sweet affection is so greatly appreciated,
with you, there's no strife, and I feel so alleviated.

All the love that I receive from you,
is really like a dream come true.
My heart has never been so happy,
I truly believe God has sent you here, just for me.

The love we make, there's just no greater gift that
could be given,
my best life with you, is what I'm livin'.
Day and night, you're all I'm thinking of,
God couldn't have blessed me with a better love.

I'm truly blessed with one of God's best.
Your love is so pure and true, I can definitely attest.
My sunshine in the morning and my beautiful star at
night,
because of your beautiful ways, I'll be forever
holding you tight.

PASSIONATE LOVE

Chocolate covered strawberries, wine, a sensuous backrub,
lit candles all around and rose petals in the bathtub.
Romantic music playing in the background,
me caressing your body as the soap chips melt in the water, so profound.

Kisses on your sweet, soft, succulent lips,
my hands complimenting your beautiful hips.
I'm starring into your pretty brown eyes,
as my appetite for you is rapidly growing, that's no surprise.

Over your screams of passion, aloud, the lion in me roars,
my way of professing that making love to you feels good, and I'm all yours,
because I just love making love with you,
it's one of my favorite things to do.

I have many ways of keeping you enticed and interested,
because I know that making love isn't always done in bed-
even walking while holding hands and a sweet conversation,
can sometimes provide some good stimulation.

Pulling your hair to the side so I can plant chocolate
kisses on your neck,
and dragging my tongue around your ear to put your
heart in check.
These electrifying feelings I have for you, I'll put
nothing before or above,
because there's just nothing else sweeter than, this
passionate love.

IT'S YOUR LOVE

That feeling in my heart, warm and overjoyed,
that place in my life, where you filled the void.
That feeling of comfort, when I needed it the most,
it's your love, about it, I brag, and boast.

LOVE NOTE

To the best girlfriend ever,
thank you for always assuring me that our love will
always be forever.
I appreciate the good feelings you always make me
feel,
constantly solidifying that what we have is real.

You truly are my BGFE,
yes, the best girlfriend ever to me.
To me you're such a breath of fresh air,
it's a blessing knowing that you'll always be there.

When it comes to girlfriends, you're so unlike any
other.
I appreciate the love and respect you show my
mother,
just by simply always greeting her by her name,
that shows me you have long term plans, thank you,
what a change.

I appreciate how our love has transcended,
both of our once-broken hearts have truly been
mended.
So fortunate that we were friends first,
I enjoyed courting you, I'll always respect you and I
know your worth.

It's so passionate, the love we make,
I've been so enticed by you, ever since the first
date.
You give the sweetest kisses and the best hugs,
your touches, so sweet, so gentle, you also give the
best backrubs.

You're that beautiful blessing that I've been asking
God for,
now that I have you, I want for nothing more.
My love, I just wanted to thank you, for helping to
keep our love afloat,
and I wish I could be there to see your reaction,
when you read this, love note.

JUST BECAUSE

Always the apple of my eye, my sweet sensation,
girl today is a celebration.
No, it's not your birthday or our anniversary,
and to celebrate us, it doesn't have to be.

So take these roses, they're beautiful, just like you,
you already have my heart, and you know that's
true.
Together we have so much love and trust,
it's something new for me, that's why I just love us.

I got you some sexy Victoria Secret under ware,
you can model them for me, and I'll take them off
you, during our private affair,
but that will be later on tonight,
after the plans that I've made for us, everything is
going to be just right.

I got some more sweet-smelling lotions from Bath
and Bodyworks for you,
I just love how they always smell so good, on you.
I know what you're thinking, stop spending money,
but baby this is just a little something for my honey.

I'm taking you to Rocklands Farm, our favorite winery,
to sip on something sweet and take in some beautiful scenery,
you can wear these cute Michael Kors sandals I bought for you today,
they'll go with any of your pretty little outfits, they always take my breath away.

I made reservations for us at Ruth's Chris Steak House for dinner,
yes, just because, I want you to know that you picked a winner,
I don't ever need any holiday to show my appreciation for you,
I do these things randomly just because, I love you.

INTOXICATING LOVE

I'm so drunk off this love, that's no doubt,
and they say, when you're drunk, the truth comes
out.
Well girl, here's my truth:
I love you to death, my verbal and physical
affection is the proof.

See, we're lovers, lovers make love,
that's what we're made of,
besides other wonderful things in our relationship,
that's what we do,
and I couldn't imagine loving on anyone else, but
you.

The way my name drips from your pretty lips,
makes me want to grab you by the hips,
and all over you, plant my kisses.
Intoxicating love, that's what this is.

I love how our eyes dance together,
makes me wonder, can this get any better?
I love how we seem to end up making love almost
every time we kiss,
It's that strong wine called love, and I could get
used to this.

When you spread your pretty wings,
I get even more intoxicated, because I see such
beautiful things.
See I'm drunk off your sexy body,
how it makes me feel, you just have no clue of what
it does to me.

I get drunk off the way you talk,
you sound so sexy, you're so beautiful, the way you
walk.
I get drunk off the scent you wear,
it's so alluring, girl I'll follow you anywhere.

You'll never know how much I cherish your smile,
which is prettier than the Jewel of the Nile.
How you love and care for me dearly,
I know how much you appreciate me, clearly.

With this love, neither one of us will ever have
taken a loss,
because one thing is for sure, I'm drunk off this
sauce,
and for me, there's just no debating,
this love, it's intoxicating.

YOU'LL NEVER KNOW

My love, you are the only woman, who has control
over my heart,
you're thoughtful, beautiful, sexy, hardworking, and
very smart.
Those are just a few things,
about you, that make my heart sing.

I'm loving you too much, I over love, that's my
problem, it's true,
my heart is very much open and vulnerable, but
only for you.
My love, you have the power to crush my world,
I gave that power to you, when I fell deeply in love
with you, girl.

See, you just don't know, you truly are wonderful,
and at times you can be so bashful.
I know you don't know how to take the sweet
nothings I say,
for you to one day understand and accept them, I
pray.

See, I just love praising your accomplishments,
so please don't ignore my compliments.
The sweet things I say to you,
I really mean them, my feelings about you are
nothing but true.

Your body is so sexy to me, my eyes see no flaws,
that's why I'm always ready to touch you, with my
brown paws,
and even with no makeup on, I adore your pretty
face,
whenever you smile around me, it lights up our
intimate space.

You make it too easy for me to show my affection,
for you, my heart will always have a sweet
confession,
I wish you knew just how much I love you,
I can honestly say, you have no clue.

Now there is a way, that I could give you a clue and
make you understand,
but I have patience, and we have time, until then,
I'm still your man.
These feelings I have will just continue to grow,
but how much I love you, for now, you'll never
know.

LOVE BIRDS

This woman right here by my side,
I give her all the love I have inside.
She's the best part of me, I can't deny,
and I just happen to be, the apple of her eye.

Two crazy love birds, that's all we are,
she's the best girlfriend ever by far.
Some say we're so overzealous,
I say, they're all just jealous.

What we have is far from any kind of spectacle,
what we have is something beautiful, something
special.
We're both enjoying this love and life,
nothing but good times and no strife.

We're both so very affectionate,
though we're not perfect,
but we warm each other's hearts for sure.
This love is so real and pure.

Gentle kisses on her neck and behind her ear,
that's every time she comes near,
we're just always touching, kissing and hugging,
always, on each other, we're just loving.

She's sweet on me like syrup on pancakes,
together we keep this love growing, we both do
whatever it takes.
When it comes to expressing our love, we always
use the sweetest words,
we'll just always be, two crazy love birds.

LOVERS

Two hearts that become one,
sharing everything under the sun.
Feelings that mirrored each other from the start,
mutually protecting each other's heart.

Praying together to God above,
to send blessings down on our love.
When you both practice vows way before the altar,
because you're that much in love, without any
falter.

When past relationships stop being referenced or
mentioned,
you've let them go, and you're giving the love you
have now, your full attention.
When every kiss is passionate,
and you're aware of each other's worth, knowing
you're both fortunate.

when you're both aware that love is always in
season,
meaningful gifts are given, just because, no reason.
Showing love and respect for each other's family,
falling deeper in love each day, gradually.

When you can set each other's soul on fire,
and always make love, satisfying that burning
desire.
Always giving your all for each other,
sharing something beautiful, lovers.

THIS IS THAT LOVE

When it comes to making love,
she's the only one I'm thinking of.
Half the time she initiates it and the other half I
initiate,
now this is the kind of love I deserve and
appreciate.

I can't say I've had hits and misses,
all I know is with her, lots of hugs, touching and
kisses.
She's definitely my first ever hit, hit right out of
sight,
finally, it's about time I got it right.

We both love doing things together and apart,
sharing family and friends, having a good time, she
really has my heart.
Sincerely she wants to be with me, she really does
care,
she lets me know that I'm her man, and not
just…there.

She doesn't just, love me,
her affection clearly lets me know that she's, in love
with me.
When she says she loves me, she means it, always
says it passionately, I adore that,
she's doesn't say it, loosely, or to just be saying it
back.

I'll always be the best that I can be,
for her, that's very important for me.
From me, my queen deserves nothing less,
so it's a must that I give her nothing but my best.

She always makes me feel wanted, finally, it feels
good,
because there was a time, my love was taken for
granted and misunderstood.
She knows that to make what we have last,
we must focus on us and our future and not re-read
our past.

This is that love,
that I've always dreamed of,
two positive and beautiful souls,
sharing and wanting the same love goals.

TO BE LOVED

To be loved, to be cared for,
to be adored, to be cherished - could you ask for
anything more?
There's just no other greater feeling,
than to have someone feel like they can dance on
the ceiling.

The warmth of a beautiful heart,
comforts so good and shows like an amazing piece
of art.
The special bond between two,
knowing that what they have is faithful, honest, and
true.

To be loved, one of the best feelings in the world,
true love, reciprocating love, with my best friend,
my lover, my girl.
Our feelings may not equally match,
but without a doubt, to each other, we'll both be
giving so much back.

Even if gone for a day, to be missed,
to have a meaningful, passionate kiss.
To be loved for the right reasons,
and to stay in love for many seasons.

Who wouldn't want to be loved and adored?
For too long my heart has been ignored,
but I know my queen is out there,
somewhere preparing herself for me, somewhere.

I have so much love that I want to give,
for love, that's why I live,
and I have loved,
but now what I want, is to be loved.

GOOD MORNING, LOVE

I'm making you cheese grits, turkey bacon, biscuits
and fresh eggs,
for you my love, but it's not because you have such
amazing legs.
I just wanted to start our day and morning off right,
replenishing our bodies from making love all night.

After breakfast, I'll clean up everything in the
kitchen,
then back to the bedroom, because for you, I have
this crazy addiction.
We'll spend about a half hour in the shower, and
you already know,
after that, I'll lotion your body from head to toe.

We'll take a nice morning walk holding hands,
enjoying the cool morning breeze, as we talk about
future plans.
See, I never thought that you would play such a
major part,
in bringing so much love and joy into my heart.

When it comes to our love, it seems that we both
have our feet planted,
and I can promise you that, I'll never take your love
for granted.
It's so easy to see that forever is in both of our eyes,
and our hearts will be forever synchronized.

I look forward to waking up to your pretty face
every morning,
for the rest of my life, yes, I believe our future will
be very rewarding,
every morning before reaching for my phone or
even making love,
I promise to always start the day by saying to you,
good morning, love.

MY WORLD

Some people want the world,
me, I just want that one special girl,
because I would have the world, if she were in my
arms.
I long to have that special girl in my arms.

My special girl will complete me,
I just know she would, I'm destined to see.
I'm ready to risk my heart for it all,
I'm even ready and willing to take down my
protective wall.

My world would be full of bright days,
gentle heat from the sun's rays,
well the heat from my heart really,
with the burning desire I'll have for her, she'll feel
me.

My world, my everything, my precious love,
She'll be everything sweet that I can think of.
I'm trusting God to do his job,
to my world, I'll be her only heart throb.

Someone I can confide in,
that will be my world, my new best friend,
in Gods timing, I'm patiently waiting for that
special girl,
God willing, she'll be so beautiful, my world.

MAKING LOVE TO ONLY YOU

Knowing that our love is unconditional,
sometimes I get so emotional,
because I'm so happy just being with you.
Making love to you, is a pleasure for me to do.

You're all things beautiful, inside and out,
I'm so very attracted to you, without a doubt.
Girl, I've never adored a body so much,
to where I constantly melt, every time and every
part I touch.

Your screams of passion,
while the waves were crashin',
as we made love in our ocean front suite,
cool breeze coming through screened doors, we
made our own heat.

Your mind is clear, there's nothing else you're ever
thinking of,
besides us, whenever we make love.
The day you professed that to me,
all the love in your heart, was all that I could see.

When making love, you, being happy, vocal, worry
free with no stress,
I can see it's got you performing at your best,
and that makes it easier for me to make
you……well, take you to ecstasy,
as I also fill you with nothing but glee.

Stimulating and meaningful conversations,
being around you, feeling good vibrations,
keeps me constantly falling for you,
girl, I'll be forever, making love to only you.

SEXY YOU

To not call you sexy would be so absurd,
with your killer coke bottle curves,
your full, luscious, sexy lips,
that are all mine and only for me to kiss.

Your skin is just the softest I've ever felt,
girl with every touch, I just melt,
just like the chocolate kisses I place on your neck,
your back and all over your chest.

My eyes are always full looking at your sexy thighs,
I get lost looking into your big beautiful eyes.
I love running my hands through your sexy long
dark hair,
and that's my favorite scent, that you always wear.

Always just a t-shirt and thongs when you lay in our
bed,
you know damn well what's always going through
my head.
When we make love, you whisper your screams of
passion in my ear,
intensely, every time I pull you near.

The way you keep yourself, fit and in shape, you
never disappoint,
toes and fingernails always stay on point.
Sexy and smart with more than one degree,
a phenomenal woman, that's what I see.

It's more than just your sexy body that does it for
me,
It's also how you're so involved in your family.
You're so very kind, very giving,
I'm so infatuated with you and the way you're
living.

I truly understand why every man is after my girl,
so glad that you want to stay trapped in my world.
What you do to me, I know, no other woman can
do.
Girl no one compares to, sexy you.

HER KISSES

Her kisses, always so sweet,
the first one knocked me off my feet.
Clearly, I remember,
it was last year, early December.

I just love her lips,
they are the sweetest I've ever kissed,
and always, kissing her is so special,
I just love it when our tongues wrestle.

I love when she touches me with those fingertips,
and guides me to those pretty lips.
I could kiss her whenever or wherever,
even outside in the worst of weather.

I'm so infatuated with kissing her lips,
whenever I do, my heart just skips,
because I just love kissing her,
that's one of my favorite things to do, with her.

I'm so glad those lips belong to me, all mine,
so glad she accepts my kisses, all the time.
With her, there's never any type of rejection,
because she also enjoys, this type of affection.

She knows that I'm a kisser,
and every time we kiss, my heart grows a little
bigger.
There are so many things I love about this beautiful
Miss,
but one of them for sure is, her kisses.

RELATIONSHIP AFFIRMATIONS

I

Allow yourself to be loved on, make time to be loved on and appreciate when your partner wants to love on you.

In your relationship, you must allow yourself to be loved on by your partner, accept those compliments, the touches, the real kisses and the looks they want to give at times. They are smiling at you because they love you and they like what they see, they are admiring your beauty. Those are just other ways of saying…I love you. Stop and make time to accept those things, sometimes the joy is seeing your reaction to those things. It doesn't take much time to just stop and say...thank you or let them know you appreciate it. If you can't spare 2 to 3 minutes for hugs, kisses and compliments, then something is not right in your relationship. Last, appreciate when you are loved on by your partner, they are simply trying to adore you or make you feel good. Appreciate the fact that they are wanting to love on only **YOU**. Would you want them to love on someone else? No, that wouldn't be right. Accept that love, always, they're wanting to make you happy or wanting to keep you happy in the relationship. So, take those words and touches, they're for **YOU** and only **YOU**.

II
Knowing your partners love language, could possibly help in making your relationship healthy and happy.

In order to speak your partners love language, you must first…. **REALLY** want to speak it. Early in your relationship you should find out what your partner's love language is. Love language is simply things that you may do for your partner that they really like, things that may help to keep them in love with you, things that simply make them happy. It's a great love communication, it's basically another form of saying…. I love you, I want to be with you and I'm happy with you. First, you must want to do those things or thing, to make them happy. Yes, sometimes it could just be…one thing. Second, it should make you feel good to do those things. Third, it **SHOULD** be reciprocated, they should learn to speak your love language as well. For example, from time to time or more often your partner may want to be taken out to eat, kissed on the neck, held or touched in a loving way, a back or foot massage, help cleaning or cooking, holding their hand, complimented, or maybe even just…making love, that right there alone is a very beautiful language, but your love language is **YOUR** love language.

It's simply what you like, it could be the thing or things that helps to keep you in your relationship. After you find out what that love language is, and if you think you'd be comfortable doing them or it, **YOU** should **WANT** to do those things or thing. Also, do those things to assure them that you're not going **ANYWHERE**. Sometimes couples speak the same love language and sometimes they don't but learning your partners love language really could help to keep or make your relationship healthy and happy.

III
No relationship will ever be perfect, but you must make sure it's worth it.

If you're looking or waiting for the perfect relationship, you may be single for a very long time. In every relationship there's always going to be something, things happen, arguments, disagreements or whatever. You'll have good days and bad days. Now, if you're in a relationship and you start to see situations you dealt with in your past, then you already know how it may end. If you were not willing to deal with those situations or issues before, you're most likely not willing to deal with them again. You must know your worth **AND** when to leave. What are you getting out of this relationship? You must ask yourself that, it's important, you do not want to waste your time or anyone else's. What you expect out of the relationship should be established in the beginning. Know that one of you in the relationship is always going to produce more, feelings, affection, material things or whatever. Sometimes one person may love a little more than the other. It's not always going to be 50/50 exact, that's **VERY** rare, but it shouldn't be a huge slant either. Make the relationship - **YOUR** relationship - make sure it's the type of relationship you both want to endure, make it worth it. Do things that they like to do, and they should do things that you like to do. You may not like all the same things but try to at least do some of the things, again, make it worth it!!

IV

IF, you pray together, and grow... together, you will not grow... apart.

If you put God first in your relationship and be faithful to God in your own spiritual way, you will both be blessed. Pray with the one you love, if not all the time, at least do it sometimes, that's a beautiful thing. Also, be willing to be pulled down to pray by the one that loves you. Keep God in your relationship, use God to help you to stay on track in your relationship. Sometimes people say, in their previous relationship, they broke up because they "grew apart," but did you ever grow together? Sometimes in the beginning, people get so caught up in fake talk aka BS, receiving expensive gifts, and/ or great sex. PAY ATTENTION to all red flags, and there's so much more to growing together than those few things. Sometimes people rely on just those things and they "grow apart." As you start your new relationship, it's a beautiful thing to be happy in the beginning, but keep that happiness going as best as you can. It will never be perfect, but it should always be worth it. Pay attention to your relationship, always. Sometimes you grow apart because you're not paying attention! When or if you sense that something is or may be wrong, question it, talk about it. Communication is the key, that may keep you from "growing apart." So, pray together and stay together, do not grow...apart.

46

V

It's not about your PAST, it's about your present.

You can't hold on to your past and your present at the same time. Sometimes in a relationship, there may be someone not willing to give up or let go of past relationships. Even if the relationship ended badly for whatever reason, they may feel the need to stay in contact somehow: social media, phone calls, e mails or texts. That's not fair to the new person they are with currently. How can you be in love, fall in love or be deeply in love with someone new if you can't let go of someone or people from your past? You should commit 100% into the person you're with now, the person you want to grow with now, if you have long term plans with them anyway. If they are important to you, make you feel special, treat you like they know your worth, or if things are different than any of your past relationships, then you should be able to let go of your past relationships. Accept that your past has taught you a lesson and you have someone good now. Enjoy that blessing.

Now, if you're co-parenting young children with someone from your past, having their phone number is not a crime….to co-parent, but that's all you should have and that's all you should need. Forgive, but **NEVER** forget and remember, their actions are the reason you moved on.

There's no need to keep up with them any other way, unless there's some kind of amicable reason that you and your current partner agree on, something that you're **BOTH** comfortable with. Keeping up with them in any other way, may make your current partner feel uncomfortable. If you can't let go for that reason, then you can't fully commit to them, you can't say you're totally or deeply in love with them. Let go of your past, focus on the relationship that's in front of you and you could have a beautiful future with them, **IF**, you're able to let go of your past. be happy with them, especially if they're happy with you and willing to do almost anything to make you happy. So, at some point you must let go of your past relationship or relationships.

VI

Treat your NEW relationship like….a NEW relationship.

Treat your **NEW** relationship like….a **NEW** relationship! Do things that new couples do, don't start your new relationship by: just picking up from where your last one ended. If you were in a 5, 10 or even 20 year long relationship you shouldn't carry yourself in your new relationship that way. Sometimes you may not even realize it, and it's not fair for your new partner to walk into some of your old relationship habits. Some habits that may be old for you may be new for them, things that they may want to experience with you. You should be doing a lot of holding hands, hugging, touching, kissing, and yes, even making love. Explore each other those first six months to a year, and yes there's always new things that you may find out as you go on but never start it off where your last relationship ended. Sometimes after years in a relationship, some things do seem to fade away, like the loving things that I've just mentioned. Which they shouldn't but yes sometimes they do, but when you start something new, you should start your relationship clock over again. Your new partner deserves a fresh start, you both do.

VII

Treat her like you know her worth, and you'll have heaven on earth.

Sometimes in relationships, us men may complain about our woman, we may not think they're acting right, or something is just wrong with her, whatever the reason may be. No, we are not mind readers but, if your woman is or seems unhappy, not all the time but sometimes, a surprise from us can do the trick. Send her those flowers just because, especially if you've never done it before or if it's been a long time since you have. When she comes home from work surprise her with a clean house, or her favorite meal. Make all of it yourself, even if you're not a great cook, the effort will be appreciated. Buy her something you know she's been talking about. Just do something nice that you've never done before or in a while, that could make her day, and maybe yours later. We must know their worth and treat them like we know it. If she's a good woman she'll appreciate it, and reciprocate in ways that will make you feel like you're in heaven. Sometimes it doesn't take much to change her attitude, but we must always treat them like we know their worth. Don't take a good woman for granted.

VIII
That same honey you used to get them, is the same honey you need to use to keep them.

Sometimes in our relationships, we get very comfortable, we may stop doing some of the sweet things we used to do in the beginning. Things that caught the attention of our love ones, things that made them say, *yes, I'm all in if this is how it's going to be*. It could be anything: flowers that used to be sent just because, special attention that used to be given, a great dish that used to be made, gentle touches that used to be given, meaningful talks you used to have or even making love or things that took place while making love. Some things should never stop or change, never let that pilot light in your relationship go out. Keep your partner interested, **IF** you still love them. Do what they like, be the person you were in the beginning. Yes, people do change, but that change doesn't have to be a 180-degree change, you must somehow let your partner know that you're still interested, still the same person they fell in love with in the beginning. Do things to remind them of that, even if they have to remind you, especially if they're still doing some or most of the same things that you liked about them in the beginning. Keep your relationship going in the right direction, always.

That verbal or and physical affection is **VERY** important, it could keep a person, if they really want to be kept. It's never going to be perfect, but it **ALWAYS** should be worth it.

IX
When you love, say it, show it, and mean it.

In your relationship, you can't expect your partner to be a mind reader, so **IF** you really love them, say it. Sincerely saying, "I love you," can mean and do so much for someone. It's just a reminder and it should always be how you truly feel, so it should be expressed. You also must show it. That doesn't always mean spending money, it could be spending time or some kind of special affection, you must somehow show that you truly do care. You also have to mean what you say and do, it's easy to just say you love someone, or to …just kiss them or make love to them, you must put something behind that, really mean it. Verbal or physical affection, nothing beats that, both are great, but you must do at least one of them to let your partner know how you feel. So say it, show it, and mean it!!!

X

Let your partner do what they can do and let them tell you what they do know.

Let your partner do what they can do for you. Sometimes you want them to do what they can't do, and most of the time it may frustrate you. So, let them do what they can do, whatever it may be and appreciate that because again, they are doing this for you. Let your partner tell you what they do know, listen to them and trust their word like they may trust yours. Your partner may not know everything, but what they do know, just take their word, depending on what it is and if they are telling you they know for sure because of experience or whatever the reason may be- cooking ingrediencies, a type of situation, directions, putting something together- whatever it may be that they say they know, just trust their word. Try not to second guess them all the time, because sometimes if you ask anyone else, you'll take their word without second guessing, but when your partner may say the same thing, you second guess. It's not fair to make your partner feel he or she hardly knows anything.

XI

If you ever feel that your partner is too nice, too good, or too sweet for you, then you're probably right.

Whenever you feel this way in a relationship, sometimes it means you don't know your worth or someone sees something in you that you don't. if someone is treating you like you've never been treated before or how you just really want to be treated, appreciate that, do not think that you don't deserve that. Appreciate the fact that someone is investing that love and all that comes with it, in you. If you really feel you don't deserve that, because you've gotten so used to being treated less, then you should probably let that person go, because you will not appreciate what they are doing. They will start to see it eventually, and your relationship may go downhill. You should never feel that someone is too good for you though, think about how you were treated in your last relationship. Being treated better is good. Know your worth. Kings and queens should be treated as such, good people should be appreciated and adored, ALWAYS.

XII

Why does it always take losing someone, to know what you really had?

In relationships, sometimes a good person is taken for granted: they go so unappreciated to the point they want to leave the relationship. We are all grown, and we all know right from wrong, when you have someone good in your life, that is showing you, your family, friends and kids, respect and love, you should appreciate that. When they do good things for you, wanting to put a smile on your face, there for you in good and bad times, appreciate that. When they are or have been faithful, loyal and honest since day one, appreciate that. If they always find time for you, only give their love and affection to only you, open your eyes, appreciate those things now. Sometimes when that good person leaves, you may think you'll be ok, until you start to think about them and all they've done for you, if you really loved them you would think about that. Yes, you may find someone new right away, but as they say, "The grass is not always greener on the other side." You may not ever get in a relationship where all your boxes are checked, if they have most of what you want and need, hold on to them. Those few flaws shouldn't matter, depending on what they are, perfect is very rare. Appreciate a good thing now, not when it's gone.

56

It is possible to lose someone because you took
them for granted, don't let it go that far, realize
what you have and hold on tight.

XIII
Are we playing or are we staying?

At a certain age for everyone, you must know if you're ready to be in a relationship or not, especially if you're 35 and older. "Are we playing?" does not necessarily mean you are playing games; it means you want to be honest. So, if you know you're not ready, you shouldn't approach or be approached by anyone without letting them know at some point very early, what you want and what you don't want. It's okay to say you're not looking for a relationship or anything long term, but you are willing to go out on dates and do whatever that is agreed upon mutually, with no strings attached. Something like that, but just speak the truth. Sometimes, that person may be wanting the same thing, so be honest, be grown, and be respectful, because if you're that, you just may be able to get what you want. Are we staying? Just means you're ready for a relationship, you're looking for something long term and you want to know if the feeling is mutual. Some people are at an age where there's no time for games, no just messing around or "friends with benefits." You simply want to know what's going on with the situation. So, a reasonable question to ask is, are we playing or are we staying?

XIV

The person that was meant for you, will always be for you and only you.

So, that person you share an effortless love with: you know, the person you're so madly in love with and it's a mutual feeling. Much time has passed and you're both still madly in love, well they were always meant for you. It may have taken some time for the both of you to be together, but that was Gods will. You've both been through what you've been through, the failed relationships, sleepless nights, loss of appetite and heart aches, because God was preparing you for each other. God knew it was time for you to be together, now. God knew that you would truly appreciate each other. You're able to love so effortlessly because it was in God's will. Gods timing and Gods will, always trust it. You won't have any worries or sleepless nights when you have an effortless love, because you both will effortlessly make it work. It won't be perfect, but it will be worth it. That effortless love, if you have it, you're blessed. That's real love, true love. You'll know it when you have it.

XV
Start your wedding vows now.

No, no one is rushing anything here. Just saying, when you commit or confirm to someone that you're in a relationship together, it's kind of like saying "I do" because it should be to have and to hold. You should be faithful, always and you should be there when they're sick or healthy. If they're not faithful in your relationship, how can they be faithful in your marriage? Nothing or no one is perfect. Yes, people can change, you can work on things or you cannot. Never wait until you're married to do right as some may say and think. Do right, now, from the beginning of your relationship. For richer or poorer, you should be there financially if you can since you're in that relationship together, helping each other out in any way you can. No, you don't start off your relationship thinking marriage, but that's just up to the both of you how you may think. You should however practice those wedding vows, which are basically relationship vows. The same things you will do in your relationship are the same things you will do in your marriage. In both instances it's called respect, respect your woman or man in your relationship. You must be faithful, honest, and dedicated in your relationship or marriage.

When it's time for marriage, it will just make it that much easier for the one you love to say, yes because you've proven to them what it's going to be like in a marriage while you were dating.

You should not be showing video games, tv shows or social media more attention and affection than you do your partner.

It's ok to play your video games, watch tv and be on social media. There's nothing wrong with that at all but if most of your attention or affection is going towards that and not the person you love, that's a problem. Technology is a blessing and a curse, a blessing because we can have so much info right at our fingertips on our phones or other devices. A curse at times because it can pull us away from others sometimes. Life is short, you should be spending more time loving on each other every opportunity you get. Give social media a break sometimes and hug, kiss or make love instead. Cuddling in bed **should** be more fun than playing games on your cell phone or watching tv. There's a way to do both, you must figure out a way to manage that time if you value your relationship. **You should not be holding your iPad or cell phone in bed more than you are holding your partner**. You should be able to pause that tv show or game for your partner when they want to show you some affection for a few seconds or even a few minutes.

The same way you pay attention to that tv, give your partner that same attention as well. Again, life is short, if you have someone to love on, love on them and let them love on you!! Sometimes, showing a little affection can do so much. It can make your partners day in many good ways or it could change a negative feeling or decision they were going to make in your relationship. Give your partner some attention, show them some kind of affection. Show your partner that they mean more to you than the video games, tv shows or social media.